P9-CIV-835

Originally published in Japan in 1977 under the title *Minna Unchi* by Fukuinkan Shoten Publishers, Inc.

First Chronicle Books edition published in the United States of America in 2020.

Library of Congress Cataloging-in-Publication Data available.

ISBN 978-1-7972-0264-8

Manufactured in China.

English translation by Chronicle Books LLC.
Typeset in Steagal Rough.

10 9 8

Chronicle Books LLC
680 Second Street
San Francisco, California 94107

Chronicle Books—we see things differently.
Become part of our community at www.chroniclekids.com.

VERYONE POOP

Taro Gomi

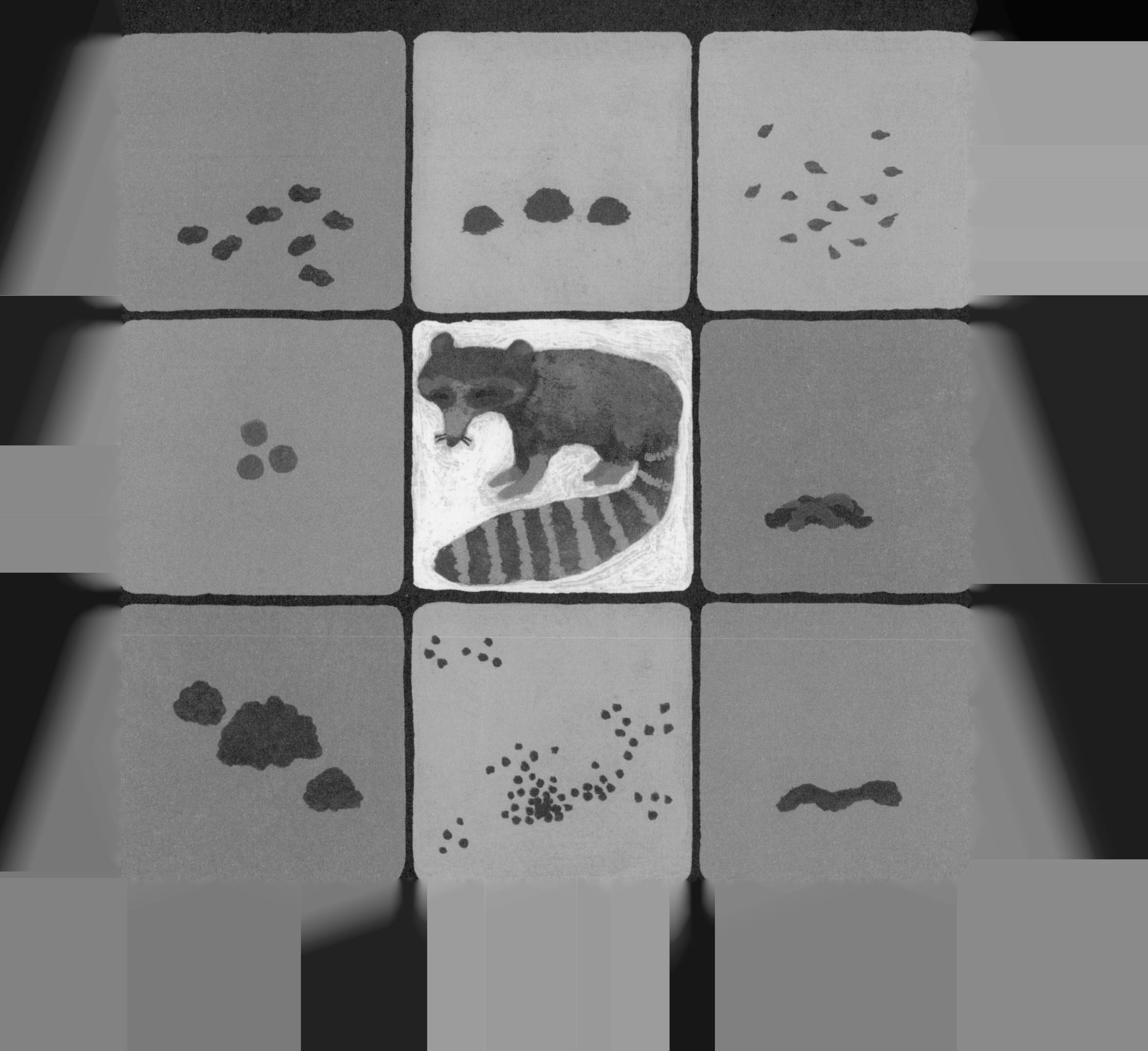

An elephant
makes a big poop.

A mouse makes
a tiny poop.

A one-hump camel makes a one-hump poop.

And a two-hump camel
makes a two-hump poop.

Just
kidding!

Fish poop,

birds poop,

and bugs
poop, too.

Different
animals
make
different
kinds of
poop.

Different shapes, different colors, even different smells!

Which end is
the snake's butt?

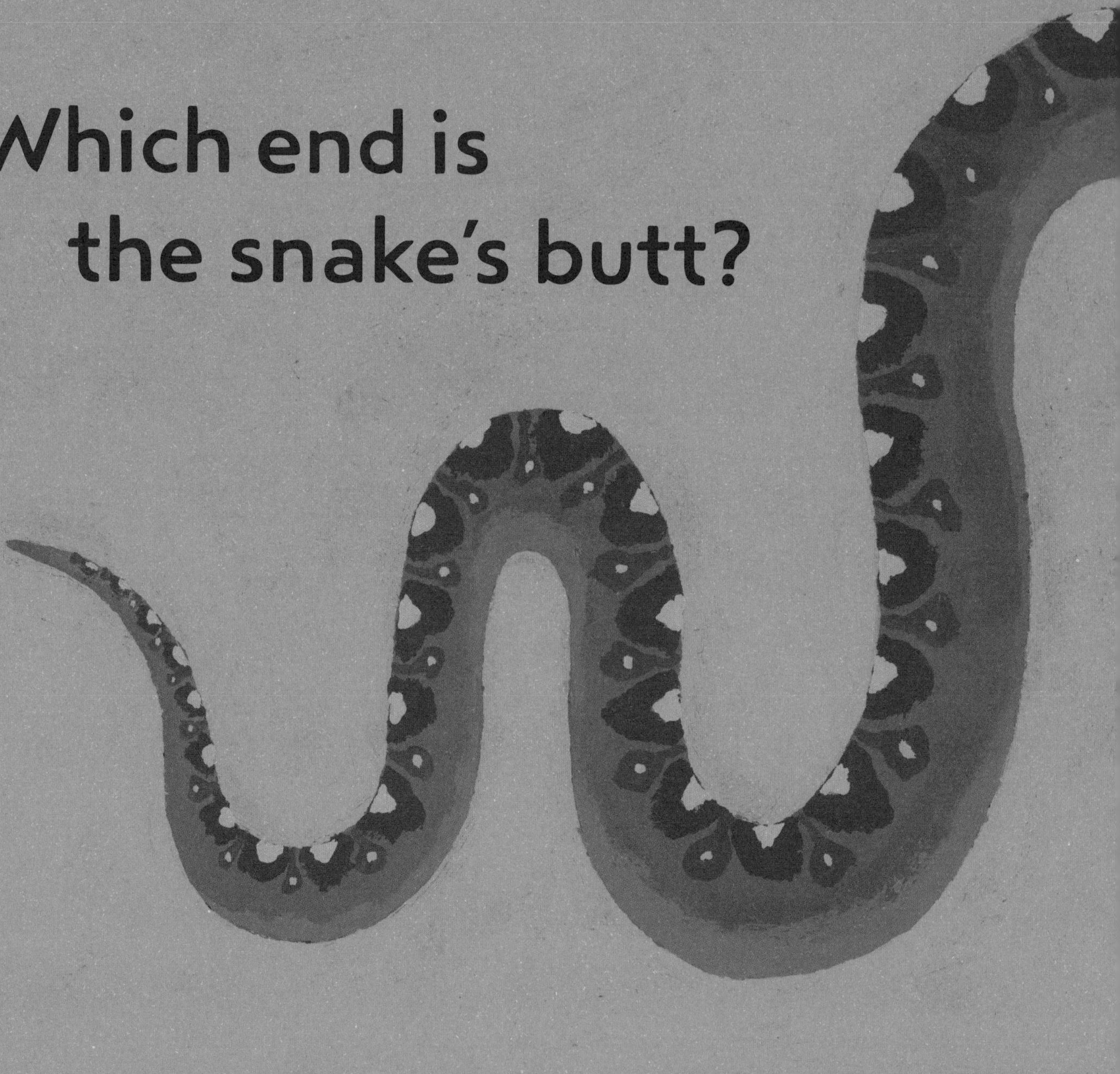

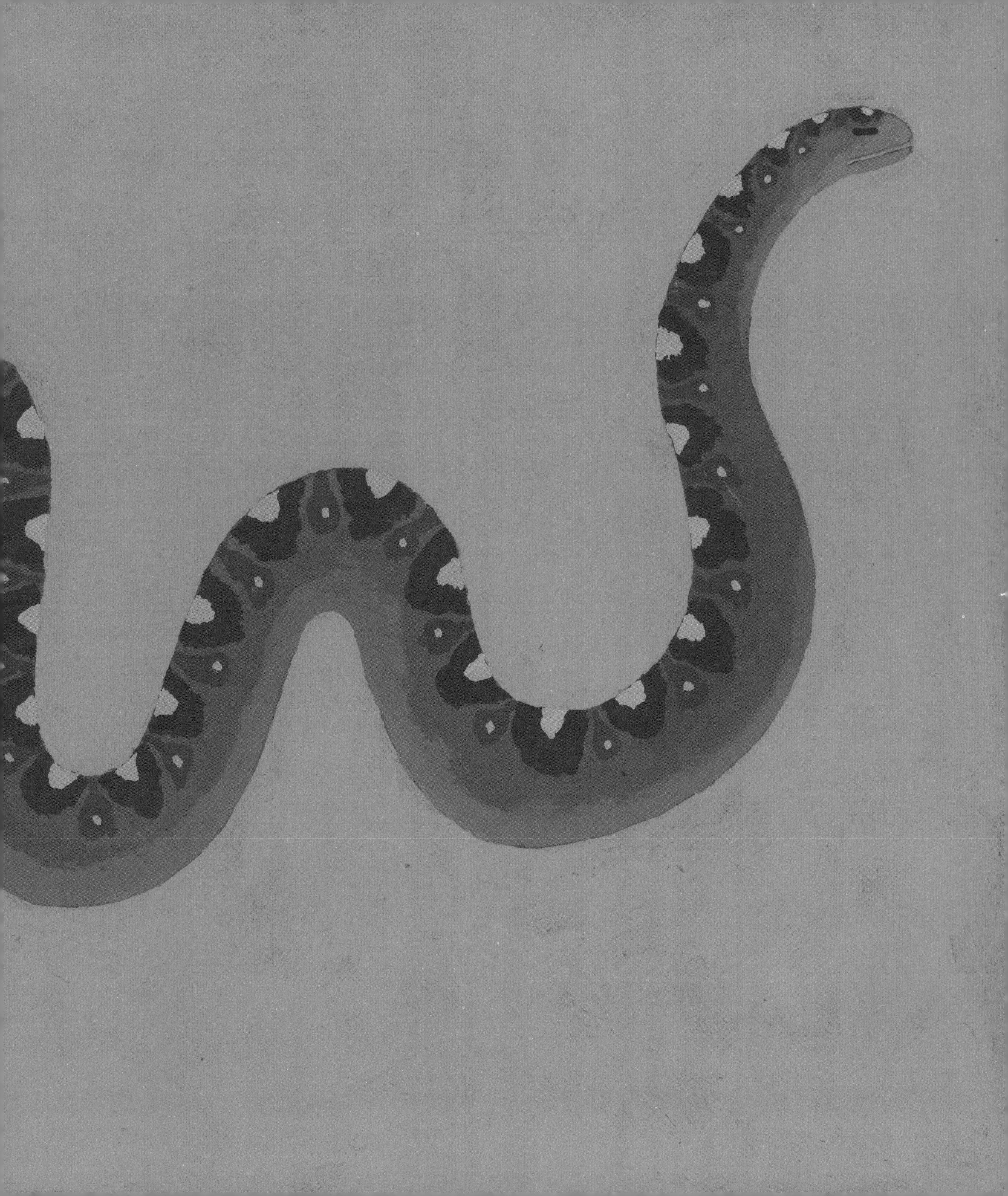

What does whale

poop look like?

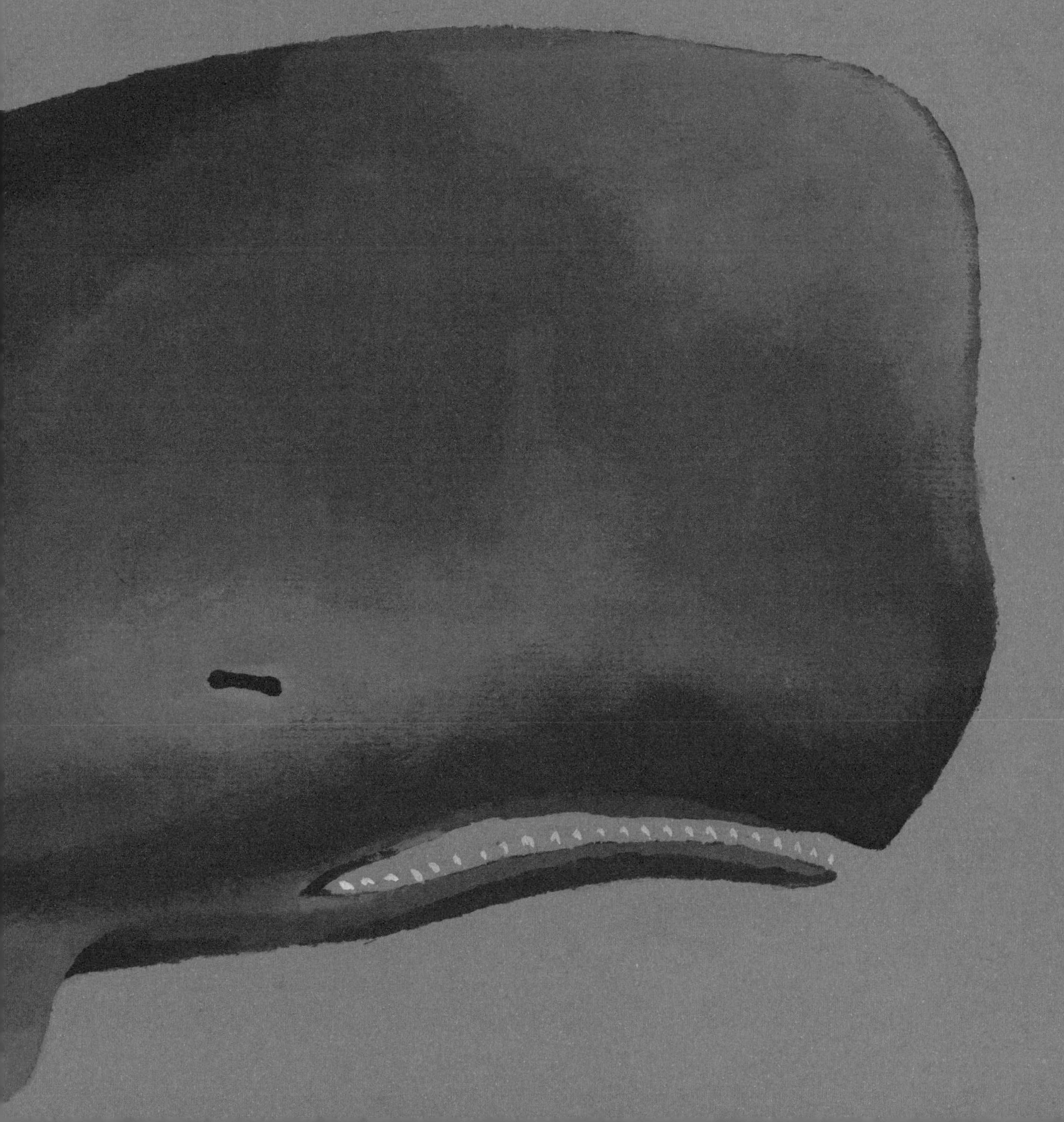

Some stop to poop.

Others do it
on the go.

Some poop
all over.

Others poop somewhere special.

Grown-ups poop.

And kids poop.

Some kids poop on the potty.

Others poop in diapers.

Some animals poop and don’t even think about it.

Some clean up
after they poop.

These animals poop by the water.

This one poops in the water.

He wipes himself with toilet paper,

then flushes it away.

All living things eat, so . . .

Everyone poops!